TEDD ARNOLD

HUGGLY'S® PIZZA

SCHOLASTIC INC.

New York   Toronto   London   Auckland   Sydney
Mexico City   New Delhi   Hong Kong

For Chris and Katie
—T. A.

ISBN: 0-439-13498-6

Library of Congress Cataloging-in-Publication Data
Arnold, Tedd.
    Huggly's pizza / by Tedd Arnold.
       p.   cm. — (The monster under the bed storybook)
    "Cartwheel books."
    Summary: Huggly and his monster friends, Booter and Grubble, set out to find the yummy human food he has tried, pizza.
    ISBN 0-439-13498-6 (pbk.)
    [1. Monsters — Fiction.   2. Pizza — Fiction.]   I. Title.   II. Monsters under the bed.
PZ7.A7379 Hy   2000
[E] — dc21
                                                                                                  99-043289

12 11 10 9 8 7 6 5 4 3   00   01   02   03   04   05   06

Printed in the U.S.A.
First printing, February 2000

"I'm hungry for pizza!" said Huggly.

His friends, Booter and Grubble, were sitting with him
in their Secret Slime Pit. They looked curiously at Huggly.

"What's pizza?" asked Grubble.

"It's a flat kind of food I once ate in the people world," said Huggly.

"It must be something monsters don't have," said Booter.

Huggly hopped up.
"Then, let's go find some!"
he said. "I'll take my
snack sack."

"Sounds good to me!" Grubble agreed. He was always
ready to eat.
"We're going on a pizza hunt!" said Booter.

The three monsters hurried to the hatchway under Huggly's favorite bed. They peeked out carefully, not wanting to be seen by any people.

"No one in sight," Huggly whispered. "They must be downstairs."

"Is that where the pizza is?" asked Grubble.

"The way I remember it," said Huggly, "the pizza came from outside. There was a knock on the door and a people person was there with pizza."

He led his friends quietly down the stairs.

They slipped out the front door without disturbing the people family.

"Okay," said Huggly. "Now everyone start looking."

The three friends searched everywhere.
"No pizza here," said Huggly.

"No pizza here," said Grubble.

"No pizza . . . wait a minute!" said Booter. "I don't even know what pizza looks like."

"Hey, that's right," said Grubble. "Neither do I."
"Don't worry," said Huggly. "I'll know it when I see it."
They crept down street after street, looking high and low.

Suddenly, Huggly cried out,
"TIME FOR PIZZA!"
   Before them was a brightly lit
building. A sign on the roof glowed
with something round and flat.

On tiptoes, the three friends peered through the window.
"Pizza-a-a-a-a," drooled Huggly.
"How do we get some?" asked Grubble. "We can't just walk in the front door."
"Let's look around back," Booter suggested.

Behind the building they found a people machine with a large pizza on top.

"That's the biggest pizza I ever saw!" said Huggly. The three of them scrambled onto the machine.

"TIME FOR PIZZA!" they all cheered, and started to chew.

"Ouch!" said Booter. "This pizza is kind of tough."
"I don't think I like it," muttered Grubble.
"Hey, this isn't real pizza!" said Huggly.

At that moment, a door on the back of the building flew open and a people person hurried out with a stack of large, flat boxes. "Everybody hide!" Booter whispered.

The people person jumped into
the machine, dropped the boxes onto
the seat beside him, and drove away
fast. Very fast!

His wheels screeched around corner after corner. All at once, he skidded to a stop. He grabbed the top box and jumped out.

"Is he gone?" Huggly asked. "I think so," said Booter. "Hey, what smells so good?"

Huggly lifted the lid on the top box and licked his lips.
"TIME FOR PIZZA!" they cheered. Booter and Grubble both
reached for a piece.

"Oh! I just remembered," Huggly said. "Monsters aren't
supposed to take people stuff. I suppose that means we shouldn't
eat people stuff either."

"What?" said Grubble. "After all this, we can't even taste it?"

They stared at the pizza and their mouths watered. Suddenly, to their surprise, the door opened beside the stack of pizzas. A strange people person reached in, grabbed the boxes, and ran off with them.

"STOP!" yelled Huggly. "That pizza isn't yours!"
Without thinking, he leaped out of the machine and
chased after the stranger.

"Huggly! Come back!" cried Booter. She and Grubble
followed him.

The people person heard the shouting and looked back. Three monsters were chasing him! "*Aiee-e-e-e-e!*" he screamed. He threw the pizzas at them and ran faster. The boxes rained down on the monsters and they tumbled to the ground.

Someone came running behind them.
"Quick, into the bushes!" said Booter.
"Thief, thief!" called the pizza person, running
up the street and shaking his fist at the stranger.

But he stopped at the pile of boxes. "Oh, no," he groaned. "I guess I'll have to go back to the shop for some fresh pizzas." He threw the whole mess into a trash bin before he left in his machine.

Huggly, Booter, and Grubble crawled out from their hiding place. They looked at the trash bin. "I guess if people throw stuff away, we can have it," said Huggly.

They looked at each other, then cheered, "TIME FOR PIZZA!"

They ate and ate and ate.

Booter and Grubble discovered they loved pizza as much as Huggly did.

Finally, there was only one box of pizza left. But they couldn't eat another bite.

"Let's take it back with us," said Huggly.
The three monsters found their way
back to the people house where they started.
But the house was dark inside and the door
was locked.

"How are we going to get inside and under the bed?" asked Huggly.

"You could climb that tree, Huggly, crawl along the roof, slide down the chimney, and unlock the door," said Grubble.

"Better yet," said Huggly, "we can build a catapult and shoot you through that open window, Grubble. Then *you* can let us in."

"Hush," said Booter. "You two hide
by the door and wait for me." Booter
set the pizza box on the edge of the porch.
Then she knocked on the door.

Huggly gasped. "What are you doing?!"

"Just be quiet," said Booter, and she hid, too.

A sleepy people father opened the door and scratched his chin. "I don't remember ordering pizza," he mumbled. "Better put it in the fridge." He stepped out onto the porch to get the box.

Behind him, the three monsters tiptoed into the house unnoticed. They raced upstairs and under the people child's bed.

"Pizza is great," said Grubble, back at the Secret Slime Pit.

"Yeah," Booter agreed. "I'm ready for more. Too bad I had to leave it on the porch."

"What you left on the porch," said Huggly, "was an empty box. The pieces of pizza fell out on the way home." He opened up his snack sack.

"TIME FOR PIZZA!"